To Mrs. Hickey
from
Melanie 1963

TISTOU
OF
THE
GREEN THUMBS

Illustrated by Jacqueline Duhème

MAURICE DRUON

TISTOU
of the Green Thumbs

TRANSLATED
by Humphrey Hare

CHARLES SCRIBNER'S SONS *New York*

To my friend,
DOM JEAN-MARIE

TISTOU
OF
THE
GREEN THUMBS

CHAPTER ONE

In which the Author
has some very important things
to say
about the name of TISTOU

T ISTOU
is a very odd name indeed and you won't find it in any
Dictionary of Proper Names. There isn't even a Saint
Tistou.

Nevertheless, there was a little boy whom everyone
called Tistou. . . . And this needs some explanation.

One day, very soon after he was born, when he
was still only about the size of a bread roll in a baker's
basket, his godmother, wearing a long-sleeved dress,
and his godfather, wearing a black hat, took the little
boy to the church and told the priest that he was to be

called Jean-Baptiste. Like most babies who find themselves in this particular situation, the little boy screamed his protests and became quite red in the face with dismay. But, like all grown-ups, who never understand babies' protests and have a habit of clinging to their ready-made ideas, his godparents merely insisted that the child was to be called Jean-Baptiste.

Then the godmother in her long sleeves and the godfather in his black hat took him back to his cradle. But a very strange thing happened. The grown-ups suddenly discovered that they were quite unable to utter the names they had given him, and they found themselves calling him Tistou.

But this is not really so very strange. How many little boys and girls are baptized Anatole, Susan, Caroline or William and are never called anything else but Tolo, Susie, Caro or Billy?

This simply goes to show that ready-made ideas are badly made ideas, and that grown-ups *don't really know what our names are*, any more than they know, although they pretend they do, where we come from, why we are in the world, or what we are here to do in it.

This is a very important thought and requires further explanation.

If we have been put into the world merely to become a grown-up, our heads, as they grow bigger, very easily absorb ready-made ideas. And these ideas, which have been made for a long time, are to be found in books. So if we read, or listen attentively to people who have read a lot, we can very soon become a grown-up like all the others.

It is also true that there are many ready-made ideas about almost everything, and this is very convenient because it means we can change our ideas quite often.

But if we have been sent into the world on a special mission, if we have been charged with the accomplishment of some individual task, things are not quite so easy. The ready-made ideas, which other people find so useful, simply refuse to stay in our heads; they go in at one ear and come out at the other, fall on the floor and get broken.

Thus we are liable to surprise our parents very much indeed, as well as all the other grown-ups who cling with such determination to their ready-made ideas!

And this was precisely the case of the little boy who had been called Tistou without anyone having asked his permission.

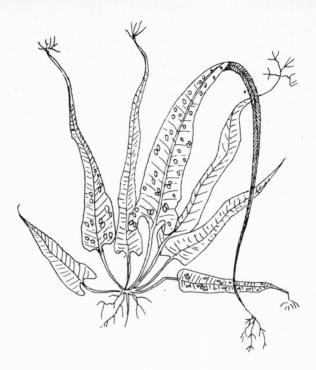

CHAPTER TWO

Introducing TISTOU,
his Parents
and the Shining House

Tistou's hair
was fair and curly at the ends. Imagine sunbeams end-
ing in little curls where they touch the ground. Tistou
had wide blue eyes and fresh, rosy cheeks. People
kissed him a lot.

Grown-ups, particularly those with wide, black
nostrils, wrinkles on their foreheads and hair growing
out of their ears, are always kissing rosy-cheeked little
boys. They say the little boys like it; but that is another
of their ready-made ideas. Really, of course, it's the

grown-ups who like it, and the little rosy-cheeked boys are very kind indeed to give them so much pleasure.

Everyone who saw Tistou exclaimed, "Oh, what a beautiful little boy!"

But this did not make Tistou conceited. Beauty seemed to him a perfectly natural quality. He was always surprised that every man, woman and child should not be as beautiful as were his parents and himself.

For we must say at once that both Tistou's parents were very beautiful indeed; and it was from looking at them that Tistou had fallen into the way of thinking that it was quite normal to be beautiful, while ugliness seemed to him both exceptional and unjust.

Tistou's father, who was called Mr. Father, had black hair brushed carefully smooth with brilliantine; he was very tall and very well dressed; he never had so much as a speck of dust on the collar of his coat and he smelled of Eau de Cologne.

Mrs. Mother was slender and had fair hair; her cheeks were as soft as rose-petals, and when she came out of her room there was a scent of flowers all round her.

Tistou was really a very lucky boy, for not only had he Mr. Father and Mrs. Mother all to himself, but he had the advantages of their enormous fortune.

For Mr. Father and Mrs. Mother, as you will already have guessed, were very rich indeed.

They lived in a magnificent house several storeys high, with a flight of steps leading up to a verandah, a big staircase, a little staircase, high windows arranged in rows of nine, and turrets with pointed hats on them, while the whole thing was surrounded by a splendid garden.

Every room in the house had such thick, soft carpets that you walked on them in perfect silence. They were splendid for playing hide-and-seek, and for running on without slippers, though this was forbidden.

Mrs. Mother would say, "Tistou, put on your slippers, you'll catch cold."

But because of the thick carpets, Tistou never caught cold.

There were also splendid, highly polished brass banisters to the big staircase. They were like a huge capital S with several humps. Starting somewhere at the top of the house they seemed to plunge downward

like golden lightning to the bearskin rug on the ground-floor.

Whenever he was alone, Tistou climbed onto the banisters and hurled himself giddily downward. The banisters were his private toboggan, his flying carpet, his magic railway; and every morning Carolus, the manservant, polished them frantically till they shone.

For Mr. Father and Mrs. Mother liked everything to shine brightly and everyone took a great deal of trouble to please them.

The hairdresser, thanks to the brilliantine we have already mentioned, succeeded in making Mr. Father's hair look like a sort of helmet which reflected the light at eight different points and everyone admired it very much. While Mr. Father's boots were so beautifully brushed and polished that, when he walked, they seemed positively to throw out sparks before him.

Mrs. Mother's nails, which were polished every day, shone like little windows in the rising sun. Round Mrs. Mother's neck, at her ears, her wrists and upon her fingers, gleamed necklaces, ear-rings, bracelets and rings made of precious stones. When she went out in

the evening to a theater or a ball, all the stars of the night seemed dim beside her.

Carolus, the manservant, used a special powder of his own invention to make the banisters into the masterpiece they were. But he also used this special powder on the door-knobs, the silver candlesticks, the chandeliers, the salt-cellars, the sugar-bowls and the buckles of belts.

As for the nine cars in the garage, one had really almost to put on dark glasses to look at them. When they all went out together, and drove through the streets, people stopped on the sidewalks. It was as if the Hall of Mirrors had gone out for a walk.

"It's like Versailles!" said the more knowledgeable.

The absent-minded took off their hats, thinking it was a funeral. Smart young women took advantage of the shiny paintwork to powder their noses.

In the stables were nine horses, each more beautiful than the other. On Sundays, when there were visitors, the nine horses were brought out into the garden to decorate the landscape. The Big Black stood under the magnolia with his wife, Beautiful Mare. The pony, whose name was Gymnast, stood near the summer-house. In front of the house, on the green lawn, the six strawberry-roans stood in line; they were thorough-breds, bred by Mr. Father, who was proud of them.

The stable-boys, dressed in silks like jockeys, ran brush in hand from one horse to another, because the horse's coats had to shine too, particularly on Sundays.

"My horses must shine like jewels!" said Mr. Father to his stable-boys.

Fastidious though he was, he was a kind man; so all obeyed him to the best of their ability. And the stable-boys groomed the roan horses with such attention to the lie of each hair that their hindquarters looked like enormous rubies of exquisite cut, while their manes and tails were braided with silver paper.

Tistou adored the horses. At night he often dreamed that he was sleeping among them on the pale straw of the stables. By day he was always going to visit them.

Whenever he ate a piece of chocolate, he put the silver paper carefully aside, and gave it to the stable-boy in charge of his pony, Gymnast. For he loved

Gymnast more than all the other horses; and this was quite natural, because Tistou and the pony were just about the same height.

And so, living in the Shining House with his scintillating father and his mother, who was a nosegay in herself, among beautiful trees, exquisite cars and lovely horses, Tistou was a very happy little boy.

Making guns is a very tiring thing to do and we can't afford weaklings in our family."

For no one doubted that one day Tistou would succeed Mr. Father as head of the factory, as Mr. Father had succeeded Mr. Grandfather, whose portrait, his face framed in a gleaming beard, his hand placed on a gun-carriage, hung on the wall of the big drawing-room.

And Tistou, who was really a very good boy, set to and ate up his soup.

Bird

CHAPTER FOUR

In which
TISTOU *is sent to School*
but does not stay there long

Uɴᴛɪʟ
he was eight years old, Tistou had no experience of
school. Mrs. Mother preferred to begin her son's
education herself and teach him the rudiments of the
three Rs, which, as everyone knows, are Reading,
wRiting and aRithmetic. We must admit that the
results were not at all bad. Thanks to some beautiful
picture-books, bought specially, Tistou learned that
A stood for Ant, Anchor and Ass, B for Ball, Balloon
and Bird, and so on. As for aRithmetic, Mrs. Mother

used swallows sitting on telephone wires. Tistou learned not only to add and subtract but was even able to divide seven swallows, for instance, by two telephone wires—the answer to which is three and a half swallows per telephone wire. How half a swallow sits on a telephone wire is another matter, which all the figures in the world have never been able to explain!

But when Tistou reached his eighth birthday, Mrs. Mother came to the conclusion that she had completed her task and that Tistou must now be entrusted to a proper schoolmaster.

So Tistou was bought a school smock, new shoes which hurt his feet, a satchel, a black pencil-box with Japanese figures on the outside, an expensive book with wide lines, another with narrow lines, and Carolus, the manservant, took him to the Mirepoil School, which had a very good reputation indeed.

Everyone expected that a little boy so neatly dressed, whose parents were so beautiful and so rich, and who already knew how to divide swallows into halves and quarters, would be very good at his lessons.

Alas, alas! School had an unforeseen and disastrous effect on Tistou.

When the long lines of letters began to stride across the blackboard, when the long chains of the multiplication tables began to unroll themselves link by link with their three-times-three, their five-times-five, and their seven-times-seven, Tistou's left eye began to blink and soon he fell fast asleep.

And yet he was not stupid, or lazy, or even tired. He was really a very good boy and tried hard.

"I won't go to sleep, I won't go to sleep," Tistou said to himself.

He fixed his eyes on the blackboard and listened as hard as he could to the Master's voice. But then his left eye would start blinking again though he did everything he could not to fall asleep. He even sang to himself a pretty little song of his own invention:

What's half a swallow?
And half of that?
A leg or a wing?
An extraordinary thing!
Were it a tart,
I'd cut off a large part
And swallow, and swallow, and swallow!

There was nothing to be done. The Master's voice was a lullaby; the blackboard turned as dark as night; the ceiling seemed to whisper down to him, "Happy dreams, Tistou!" and the Mirepoil schoolroom became a land of oblivion.

"Tistou!" yelled the Master.

"I didn't do it on purpose, Sir," said Tistou, waking up with a start.

"I can't help that," said the Master. "Repeat what I've just been saying."

"Six tarts—divided by two swallows——"

"Go to the bottom of the class!"

His first day at school, Tistou got zero for everything.

His second day he was punished by being kept in for two hours. That's to say that he slept in the schoolroom for two extra hours.

On the third day the Master gave Tistou a letter for his father.

Mr. Father, when he opened the letter, was pained to read the following words: "Sir, your son is not like other people. We cannot keep him here."

The school had
sent Tistou back
to his parents.

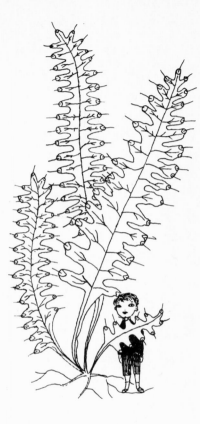

CHAPTER FIVE

In which Care
weighs upon the Shining House
and a New System
of Education
is decided on for TISTOU

Care is a form of sorrow
which oppresses one in the morning and stalks beside
one throughout the day. Care will slip into the room
when you aren't looking, hover among the leaves in
the wind, travel on bird-song, creep along bell-wires.

That morning, at Mirepoil, Care's name was:
"Not like other people."

Even the sun was reluctant to rise.

"I don't like the idea of having to wake up poor
Tistou," he said to himself. "As soon as he opens

his eyes, he'll remember he's been expelled from school. . . ."

The sun decided to take evasive action and merely emitted little tiny rays heavily lined with mist; the sky over Mirepoil stayed gray.

But Care had more than one trick in his bag; and he had an inordinate desire to be noticed. He slipped into the factory siren.

And everyone in the house heard the huge siren scream: "Not like o-o-ther pe-o-o-ple! Tistou is not like o-o-ther pe-o-o-ple!"

So Care entered Tistou's room.

"What's going to happen?" Tistou wondered. He dug his head into the pillow; but he couldn't go to sleep again. He had to admit that it was a most unfortunate thing to be able to sleep so well in school and yet so badly in one's bed!

Amelia, the cook, grumbled to herself as she lit the stove. "Our Tistou not like other people? I've never heard such nonsense! He's got two arms and two legs, hasn't he?"

And Carolus, as he angrily polished the banisters, said, "Tistou not like ozer people! Jus' let them come

and say eet to my face and see what happen' to zem!"
Carolus, it should be pointed out, spoke with a slight
foreign accent.

And in the stables the stable-boys whispered to
each other, "Not like other people, a nice boy like
that? What do you make of it?"

And since horses share the cares of human beings,
the roan thoroughbreds seemed positively irritable,
switched their tails and pulled at their halters. Beautiful
Mare had suddenly grown three white hairs on her
forehead.

Only the pony, Gymnast, seemed unperturbed and
ate his hay quite calmly, baring his beautiful white
teeth, each of which was crowned by a sort of clover
leaf.

But, apart from the pony who pretended indif-
ference, everyone was really very worried as to what
was to be done with Tistou.

And it was naturally his parents who asked themselves this question the most anxiously.

Mr. Father stood before his looking-glass making
his hair shine, but he could take no pleasure in it,
indeed was doing it only out of habit.

"The boy," he thought, "seems more difficult to develop even than a gun."

Reclining on her pink pillows, Mrs. Mother dropped a tear into her morning coffee.

"If he goes to sleep in school, how is he ever to be taught anything?" she asked Mr. Father.

"Inattention may not be an incurable disease," replied the latter.

"Dreaming is undoubtedly less dangerous than bronchitis," replied Mrs. Mother.

"But Tistou has got to grow up some time," said Mr. Father.

After this anxious conversation they fell silent a moment. They were both thinking, "What are we to do for the best?"

Mr. Father was a man of quick and bold decisions. Managing an armament factory tempers the mind. And he loved his son very much.

"It's quite simple; I know the answer," he said. "Tistou learns nothing at school; very well, he shall not go to school. Books send him to sleep; there will be no more books. Since he's not like other people, we shall try an entirely new system of education! He shall learn those things he must know by direct observation. He shall learn about stones, gardens and fields on the spot; he shall be taught the administration of town and factory, and all else that can help him to become a grown-up person. After all, life is the best school there is. We shall soon see whether it works or not."

Mrs. Mother enthusiastically approved Mr. Father's decision. She almost regretted having no other children to whom such a delightful system of education might be applied.

As far as Tistou was concerned, that was the end of having to swallow down his bread and butter in a hurry and carry a satchel about, while his desk, on which his head had so often fallen involuntarily in sleep, was a thing of the past. So was the figure 0. A new life was about to begin.

The sun shone again.

CHAPTER SIX

In which TISTOU
*has a Gardening Lesson
and discovers
that he has Green Thumbs*

TISTOU
put on his straw hat for his gardening lesson.

It was the first experiment in the new system. Mr. Father had thought it logical to begin with the garden. After all, a gardening lesson was fundamental, a lesson about the earth, the earth on which we walk and which produces the vegetables we eat and the hay upon which animals feed till they are fat enough to be eaten too. . . .

"The earth," Mr. Father had said, "is the origin and basis of all else."

"I hope to goodness I don't go to sleep again," thought Tistou as he went to his lesson.

Mr. Moustache, the gardener, having been warned by Mr. Father, was awaiting his pupil in the greenhouse.

Mr. Moustache was a lonely old man; he talked little and was not always very good-tempered. An extraordinary thicket, white as snow, grew under his nose.

How can one describe Moustache's moustache? It was one of the wonders of nature. On blustery days, as he went off with his spade over his shoulder, it was splendid to see; you might have thought he was breathing two white flames which curled up to his ears.

Tistou was very fond of the old gardener, though he was a little frightened of him.

"Good morning, Mr. Moustache," said Tistou, politely raising his hat.

"Ah, there you are!" said the gardener. "We'll see what you can do. Here's a heap of earth and some flower pots. Fill the pots with the earth, make a hole in the middle with your thumbs, and arrange the pots in a line along the wall. Then we'll put suitable seeds in the holes."

Mr. Father's hothouses were beautiful, quite in keeping with the rest of the establishment. Beneath the shelter of the shining panes of glass a big stove produced a warm, damp atmosphere; mimosas flowered in the middle of winter; palms, imported from Africa, flourished in them; there were lilies for their beauty; jasmin and tuberoses for their scent; and even orchids which are neither beautiful nor scented, were grown for a quite useless quality in a flower: their rarity.

Moustache was sole master of this part of the estate. When Mrs. Mother brought friends to visit the hothouses on Sundays, he stood politely at the door in a clean overall. He was about as talkative as a hoe.

Nevertheless, if any one of the ladies dared so much as to light a cigarette or make to touch one of his flowers, he would rush forward, crying, "Are you trying to suffocate them, strangle them to death?"

Tistou, as he performed the task Moustache had allotted him, was pleasantly surprised to find that this form of work did not send him to sleep. On the contrary, he enjoyed it. The soil smelled nice. An empty pot, a spadeful of soil, a hole with his thumbs, and he had done the trick. All he had to do was to go on to the next one. The pots fell into line along the wall.

While Tistou worked hard at his task, Moustache was walking slowly round the garden. Tistou discovered that day why the old gardener spoke so little to people: he preferred talking to his flowers.

Besides, it's obvious that if you pay a compliment to every rose on a bush or every blossom on a shrub, you won't have much voice left by the end of the day to say, "Good evening, Sir" or "Good night, Madam" or "Bless you!" when somebody sneezes—all those little phrases which make people say, "How polite he is!"

Moustache was going from one flower to another, asking them how they were.

"Well, little Tea-Rose, still up to your old tricks, eh? Keeping a few buds in reserve to flower when there's no one to see them? And you believe yourself king of the walk, morning-glory, do you? Just trying to climb up to the top of my pagoda? These are nice goings on!"

Then he turned his attention to Tistou, "What, not finished yet!"

"I've nearly finished," said Tistou. "I've only got three more pots to fill."

He quickly filled them and went to meet Moustache at the other end of the garden.

"There, I've finished."

"Well, we'll have a look," said the gardener.

They returned slowly because Moustache kept on stopping to congratulate a peony on its complexion, or encourage a hydrangea to turn blue. . . . Suddenly, they came to a halt in utter stupefaction and amazement.

"I can't be dreaming, can I?" said Mr. Moustache, rubbing his eyes. "You *do* see what I see?"

"Yes, I do, Mr. Moustache."

Under the wall, just a few yards away, every pot Tistou had filled had flowered—in five minutes!

Don't let's make any mistake about it: here was no question of merely a few, pale, hesitant shoots. Not at all. Every pot contained a huge, a splendid begonia. Together they formed a thick red hedge.

"It's unbelievable," said Moustache. "It takes at least two months to grow begonias like these!"

But a prodigy is a prodigy; one begins by establishing its undeniable existence, and then one goes on to try to explain it.

"But we didn't put any seeds in the pots, Mr. Moustache," said Tistou, "so where do the flowers come from?"

"It's most mysterious," said Moustache, "very mysterious indeed."

And he suddenly took Tistou's little hands in his own calloused ones and said, "Show me your thumbs!"

He turned his pupil's thumbs this way and that, examined them in the shade and in the sunlight.

"My boy," he said at last, after deep reflection, "something very astonishing and extraordinary has happened to you. You've got green thumbs."

"Green!" cried Tistou in surprise. "They look pink to me and, at the moment, rather dirty. They're certainly not green."

He stared at his thumbs but they looked just as usual.

"You can't see it, of course," said Moustache. "Green thumbs are invisible. It's something that happens under the skin; what's known as 'hidden talent.' Only an expert can recognize it. Well, I'm an expert, and I tell you you've got green thumbs."

"What do you do with green thumbs? What do you use them for?"

"Oh, they're wonderful things," said the gardener. "A true gift of heaven! You see, there are seeds everywhere. Not only in the earth; but on the roofs of houses, on window ledges, on pavements, fences and walls. Hundreds of millions of seeds which come to nothing. There they are, waiting for a puff of wind to blow them into a garden or a field. They often die, caught between two stones, without a chance of ever becoming flowers. But if a green thumb lights on one of them, wherever it may be, the flower grows at once. There's the proof of it, staring you in the face. Your thumbs have lighted on begonia seeds hidden in the earth, and you can see the results for yourself. Believe me, I envy you; green thumbs would have been very useful to me in my profession."

Tistou showed no apparent enthusiasm at this revelation.

"They'll say I'm not like other people again," he muttered.

"The best thing," Moustache said, "is to tell no one about it. What's the use of merely making people curious or jealous? Hidden talent often leads to trouble. You've got green thumbs, and that's a fact. Well, keep it to yourself; it'll be our secret."

And in the notebook provided by Mr. Father, and

which Tistou had to get signed at the end of every lesson, Moustache wrote:

"The boy shows promise as a gardener."

CHAPTER SEVEN

In which TISTOU
is entrusted to Mr. Turnbull,
who gives him a lesson
on Order

UNDOUBTEDLY
Mr. Turnbull's explosive temperament must have been
due to long familiarity with guns.

Mr. Turnbull was Mr. Father's manager. Mr.
Turnbull was in charge of the numerous employees in
the factory and counted them each morning to make
sure that none was missing; he looked through the
barrels of the guns to make sure that they were perfectly straight; and, in the evening, he made sure that
the doors were properly locked, often working late
into the night, to check the figures in the great ledgers.
Mr. Turnbull was a very orderly man.

Mr. Father had thought him a suitable person to continue Tistou's education the very next day.

"Today we shall have a lesson about the town and a lesson about order," said Mr. Turnbull, standing in the hall, as if he were addressing a regiment.

It must be said that Mr. Turnbull had been in the army before he had taken to manufacturing guns and, even if he had not invented gunpowder, he knew at least how to explode.

Tistou slid down the banisters.

"Go back," said Mr. Turnbull, "and come down by the stairs."

Tistou obeyed, though it seemed absurd to go up merely in order to come down again, now that he was downstairs already.

"What have you got on your head?" asked Mr. Turnbull.

"A checked cap."

"Put it on straight then."

You mustn't think that Mr. Turnbull was a wicked man; he was merely rather choleric and enjoyed getting angry over trifles.

"I should have preferred to continue my lessons with Moustache," Tistou said to himself.

But he set out side by side with Mr. Turnbull.

"A town," said Mr. Turnbull, who had taken pains to prepare the lesson, "consists, as you can see, of streets, monuments, houses, and the people who live in the houses. What, in your opinion, is the most important thing in a town?"

"The botanical gardens," said Tistou.

"Not at all," replied Mr. Turnbull. "The most important thing in a town is order. Without order, a town, a country, a whole society are merely as chaff before the wind and cannot endure. Order is essential and, in order to maintain it, disorder must be punished."

"Mr. Turnbull must be right, of course," thought Tistou, "but why does he have to shout so loudly? Here's a grown-up with a voice like a trumpet. Does order mean making so much noise?"

The passers-by in the streets of Mirepoil stopped and looked round, much to Tistou's embarrassment.

"Pay attention, Tistou. What is order?" asked Mr. Turnbull severely.

"Order? It's when one's happy."

Mr. Turnbull said, "Hm!" and his ears turned even redder than they normally were.

"I've noticed," Tistou went on, refusing to be intimidated, "that my pony Gymnast, for instance, is much happier when he's been well rubbed-down, properly groomed and has his mane braided with silver paper than when he's all covered with dirt. And I know that Moustache, the gardener, smiles on the trees when they've been properly pruned. Isn't that order?"

This answer did not seem to satisfy Mr. Turnbull, whose ears turned redder yet.

"And what happens to people who create disorder?" he asked.

"They must be punished, of course," replied Tistou, who thought that "creating disorder" was rather like "strewing his slippers" about the room or "strewing his toys" over the garden.

"They're put in prison, here," said Mr. Turnbull, indicating to Tistou with a sweep of his hand a huge, gray, windowless wall—a most uncommon wall.

"Is that the prison?" asked Tistou.

"Yes, it is," said Mr. Turnbull. "It is a monument to the maintenance of order."

They walked along the wall and came to a high, black, iron gate surmounted with spikes. And beyond the gate was a vista of further dismal walls. And all the walls and all the gates were topped with spikes.

"Why did the builder put those horrible spikes everywhere?" asked Tistou. "What use are they?"

"They stop the prisoners escaping."

"If the prison wasn't so ugly," said Tistou, "perhaps they'd feel less desire to leave it."

Mr. Turnbull's cheeks turned as red as his ears.

"What an odd child," he thought. "He's really had no education at all." And aloud, he said, "You ought to know that a prisoner is a wicked man."

"And so they put him in there to cure him of his wickedness, do they?" asked Tistou.

"They try. They try to teach him to live without stealing and without killing people."

"Surely he'd learn much quicker if the prison wasn't so ugly," said Tistou.

"Ah! Stubbornness!" thought Mr. Turnbull.

Through the gates, Tistou saw prisoners walking

silently round in a circle, their heads bowed. They looked terribly unhappy with their shaven heads, their striped clothes and their heavy boots.

"What are they doing?"

"It's their recreation hour," said Mr. Turnbull.

"Well, really," thought Tistou, "if that's what their recreation's like, what must their hours in school be! This prison is really too dismal."

He felt like crying and was silent during the whole walk home. Mr. Turnbull interpreted his silence as a good sign and thought that the lesson on order had borne fruit.

All the same, he wrote in Tistou's report-book, "The boy needs watching closely; he asks too many questions."

CHAPTER EIGHT

In which TISTOU
*has a Bad Dream and
what happens as a result of it*

CERTAINLY TISTOU
asked too many questions; he even went on asking
them in his sleep.

The night after his lesson on order, he had an
appalling nightmare. Of course, dreams are only
dreams, and their importance should not be exagger-
ated. But one can't stop oneself dreaming.

So Tistou saw in his sleep his pony Gymnast, his
head shaved, walking round and round in a circle
between high, dark walls. And behind him the roan
thoroughbreds, their heads shaved too, dressed in
striped clothes, wearily dragging their feet along in

ridiculous boots. Suddenly Gymnast, having first looked to right and left to see that no one was watching him, made a dash for the gates and tried to jump over them. But he fell back on the iron spikes. His ridiculous boots beat the air, and he neighed in the most lamentable way.

Tistou woke up with a start, his forehead was damp and his heart beating hard.

"Luckily it was only a dream," he said to himself very quickly. "Gymnast is in the stables and so are the thoroughbreds."

But he couldn't go to sleep again.

"What would be so hard on horses must be even worse for men," he thought. "Why should the poor prisoners be made to look so ugly; they won't become any the better for it. I know quite well that, if I were shut up inside there, even if I had done nothing wrong before, I should most certainly become very wicked indeed. What can be done to make them less unhappy?"

He heard eleven o'clock and then midnight strike on the Mirepoil church clock. But he went on asking himself questions.

And, quite suddenly, he had the glimmerings of an idea.

"Supposing the poor prisoners were surrounded with flowers? Order would be a less ugly thing, and perhaps the prisoners would become better. Supposing I tried my green thumbs? I'll suggest it to Mr. Turnbull. . . ."

But then he thought that Mr. Turnbull would merely turn red in the face. And he remembered Moustache's advice not to speak of his green thumbs.

"I shall have to do it alone, without anyone knowing."

Once an idea has taken possession of one's mind it becomes a resolve. And a resolve never leaves one in peace till it has been acted upon. Tistou felt that he could not go to sleep again till he had put his plan into execution.

He got out of bed and searched for his slippers; one of them had hidden itself under the chest of drawers. But where was the other? The other was laughing at him, hanging from the window-latch. That's what comes of throwing your slippers about!

Tistou crept out of the room; the thick carpet deadened the sound of his steps.

He silently reached the banisters and slid down them on his stomach.

Outside, the moon was full. The man in the moon was blowing out his cheeks with fresh air.

On the whole, the moon is kind to people who go out into the night. Hardly had he seen Tistou crossing the lawn in his long white night-shirt, than he polished up his face with a cloud that happened to be in reach of his hand.

"If I don't watch over that boy," he said to himself, "he'll end up by falling into a ditch."

The moon reappeared, brighter than ever, and even sent a message to the stars of the Milky Way asking them to twinkle as brightly as they could.

Protected by the moon and the stars, Tistou, half walking, half running through the deserted streets, reached the prison without incident.

He was a little bit nervous, of course. This was his first adventure.

"If only my green thumbs work properly!" he thought. "If only Moustache hasn't made a mistake!"

Tistou poked his thumbs wherever he could, into the earth, into the crack between the wall and the pavement, into the crevices between the stones, into the sockets of each prison bar. He worked very conscientiously. He didn't even neglect the keyhole of the entrance gate, or the sentry-box where a guard was asleep.

When he had finished, he went home and fell asleep at once.

Indeed, Carolus had considerable difficulty in waking him in the morning.

"Wake up, Tisti! Sun shine bright!" We have already mentioned the fact that Carolus spoke with a foreign accent.

There was a question on the tip of Tistou's tongue, but he dared not ask it. All the same, he did not have to wait long to know the result of his experiment.

For, goodness me, what had happened to the prison? If Mr. Turnbull had fired a big gun in the middle of Mirepoil Square, he couldn't have created more excitement! Imagine the bewilderment of the whole town at the spectacle of such a wonder! Imagine the astonishment of the people when they saw their prison transformed into a castle of flowers, into a palace of marvels!

Before ten o'clock, the whole town had heard the fabulous news. By midday the whole population was gathered in front of the high wall covered with roses and the bars transformed into arbors.

There was not a window in the prison, not a single

bar which had not received its share of flowers. Creepers climbed and clung and hung down; while the horrid spikes on the walls had been replaced by cacti.

The most odd sight of all was perhaps the sentry-box over which honeysuckle had grown so thickly that the guard was imprisoned inside. The plants had used his rifle as a prop and had blocked the entrance. The astonished crowd gazed at the guard, who was calmly and resignedly smoking his pipe in the shelter of a bower.

No one could explain the miracle. No one except, of course, Moustache, who came to have a look like everyone else and then went off without a word.

But that afternoon, when Tistou put on his straw hat for his second gardening lesson and went in search of him, Moustache greeted him with, "Oh, so there you are! Not bad, not bad at all! For a start, you've done very well."

Tistou felt rather embarrassed.

"Without you, Mr. Moustache, I should never have known I had green thumbs," said Tistou, by way of rendering thanks.

But Moustache did not like people to be effusive.

"All right, all right," he said. "But you've used too much honeysuckle. And you must beware of aristolochia. It's a fast-growing creeper but its leaves are dark. Next time, use rather more morning-glory; it'll add a note of gaiety."

Thus Moustache became Tistou's secret adviser.

CHAPTER NINE

In which the Experts
can discover nothing,
but in which TISTOU
makes a Discovery

G̲ROWN-UPS
have an extraordinary mania for trying to explain the inexplicable.

Whenever anything rather surprising happens, they get fidgety. If something new happens in the world, they become determined to prove that this new thing resembles something they know about already.

Should a volcano become quietly extinct, like the butt-end of a cigarette, a dozen bespectacled experts have to go peering, listening and sniffing about the crater, get themselves lowered into it on ropes, scratch their knees, get hauled up again, capture air in test-tubes, make drawings, write books and argue, instead of saying quite simply, "This volcano has stopped smoking; it must be extinct."

If one really comes to think of it, the experts have never really been able to explain how volcanoes work anyway!

The mystery of Mirepoil prison gave the grown-ups a splendid opportunity of getting excited. Journalists and press-photographers arrived first on the scene, because it's their professional duty, and immediately took all the rooms in the Ambassadors' Hotel, which was the only one in the town.

Then experts, the kind called botanists, arrived from all over the place, by train, air, taxi and a few on bicycles even. Botanists are people who busy themselves cutting up flowers, giving them unpronounceable names, drying them between sheets of blotting paper and watching to see how long it takes them to lose their colors.

It's a profession that requires a great deal of study.

When a lot of botanists gather together, they call themselves a congress. So there was a congress of botanists at Mirepoil. There exists an infinite variety of flowers, but only three kinds of botanists: distinguished

botanists, famous botanists and eminent botanists. They tend to call each other "Professor" or "my dear Colleague."

Since the hotel was full of journalists, who refused to vacate it, it became necessary to set up a camp for the botanists in the square. It was rather like a circus, but not such fun.

Tistou spent a very anxious time.

"If they discover that I did it," he confided to Moustache, "it's going to lead to a lot of trouble!"

"Don't you worry," replied the gardener; "those fellows don't even know how to pick a nice bunch of flowers. They won't find out, I'll stake my moustache on it."

And indeed, by the end of a week, which they spent examining every leaf and flower through magnifying-glasses, the experts had got no further. They had to admit that the flowers about the prison were like any other flowers; the only odd thing about them was that they had grown in a single night. So the experts began to argue among themselves, to accuse each other of ignorance, telling lies and creating mysteries. And now their camp really was rather like a circus.

But congresses must end with a report. Eventually, the botanists produced one, but it was full of Latin words so that no one should be able to understand it; they talked of peculiar atmospheric conditions, of little birds that had dropped the seeds and of the quite exceptional fertility of the prison walls due to certain habits of the Mirepoil dogs. Then they went off to another part of the country, where a stoneless cherry had been recently discovered, and Tistou felt safe again.

But what about the prisoners? I'm sure you want to know what they thought about it all.

Well, the excitement and astonishment of the botanists paled beside what the prisoners felt.

The honeysuckle growing in the keyholes prevented the doors being shut. But, since the prisoners were no longer aware of the bars at the windows of their cells, nor of the barbed wire and spikes on the walls, they forgot their longing to escape.

Even the most surly forgot to swear, so delighted were they with the flowers that surrounded them; even the wickedest of them forgot to get angry and fight each other. And those who were due to be

released positively refused to go: they had acquired a taste for gardening.

The Mirepoil prison was quoted as a model throughout the whole world.

And no one was more delighted than Tistou, though his was a secret triumph.

But secrets are very difficult things to keep.

When you feel happy, you want to tell someone about it, shout about it even. And Moustache hadn't always got time to listen to Tistou's confidences. So Tistou, when he felt that he really had to tell someone about his secret or burst, used to go and talk to Gymnast.

Gymnast's ears were covered with a pretty pale brown fur, which was delightfully soft to the lips. Tistou enjoyed whispering into them.

"Gymnast, listen carefully and don't tell anyone," said Tistou one morning, when he happened to meet the pony in the field.

Gymnast pricked an ear.

"I have discovered a most extraordinary thing," whispered Tistou. "Flowers prevent evil things from happening."

CHAPTER TEN

In which TISTOU
is given a lesson on poverty
by Mr. Turnbull

Sᴏᴍᴇᴛʜɪɴɢ quite out of the ordinary
has to happen for little boys to be given a holiday. A
prison that bursts into flower naturally creates a good
deal of astonishment; but grown-ups recover very
quickly from astonishment, and it's not long before it
seems quite natural to them that there should now be a
shrubbery where once there was a gray stone wall.

People become accustomed to anything, even to the
most extraordinary things.

As far as Mr. Father and Mrs. Mother were concerned, Tistou's education soon became their principal
anxiety once more.

"I think the time has now come to show him what poverty is," said Mr. Father.

"After that, he should be taught what illness means," said Mrs. Mother, "so that he may learn to take proper care of his health."

"Mr. Turnbull gave him an admirable lesson on order," said Mr. Father. "I suggest he should give him a lesson on poverty too."

Thus it was that the next day, under the auspices of Mr. Turnbull, Tistou learned that poor people live in slums.

Tistou had been told to put on his old blue cap.

In order to explain to Tistou that the slums were on the edge of the town, Mr. Turnbull used his most trumpet-like voice.

"These slums are a scourge," he declared.

"What is a scourge?" asked Tistou.

"A scourge is an evil which attacks a large number of people, a very serious evil."

Mr. Turnbull needed to say no more. Tistou was already rubbing his thumbs.

But what awaited him was a far worse sight than any prison. Narrow, muddy, evil-smelling streets wound between a hodge-podge of wooden hovels which were so tumbledown and ruinous that it was a marvel they stood up at all. The doors had all been patched either with cardboard or pieces of old packing-cases.

Lying next door to the town proper, the wealthy town built of stone where the streets were cleaned every morning, the slum was like another town altogether and did it no honor. Here there were no street-lamps, no sidewalks, no shops, no municipal watering-carts.

"A little grass would harden the mud and make these streets a great deal pleasanter; while plenty of morning-glory mingled with clematis would do a great deal to hold these tumbledown hovels together," thought Tistou, who was considering touching all the hideous things he saw.

The hovels were terribly overcrowded and, as a result, their inhabitants looked very unhealthy.

"Living huddled together without light, they turn pale like the endive Moustache grows in the cellar. I'm sure I shouldn't be happy if I were treated like an endive."

Tistou decided to grow geraniums along the window-ledges so that the slum children might at least have a little color to look at.

"But why do all these people live in these rabbit-hutches?" he asked.

"Because they haven't got proper houses, of course; what a stupid question," replied Mr. Turnbull.

"But why haven't they got proper houses?"

"Because they haven't got any work."

"Why haven't they got any work?"

"Because they've got no luck."

"So then they haven't got anything at all?"

"That's what real poverty is, Tistou."

"At least they'll have a a few flowers tomorrow," Tistou said to himself.

He saw a man beating a woman, and a child running away in tears.

"Does poverty make people wicked?" asked Tistou.

"Often," replied Mr. Turnbull, who proceeded to launch out in the most horrifying sort of sermon.

As far as Tistou could make out, poverty was like a horrible black hen, with a hooked beak and angry eyes, whose wings stretched widespread across the world, while she hatched out the most repulsive brood of chicks. Mr. Turnbull knew them all by name: there was the thief-chick, who stole and cracked safes; the drink-chick, who always had a glass in his hand till he fell down in the gutter; the vice-chick, who was always doing the most disgraceful things; the crime-chick, who was a sort of murderer armed with a revolver; and the revolution-chick, who was clearly the worst of all. . . .

"Tistou, you're not listening to me," said Mr. Turnbull. "And stop poking your thumbs into all that dirt! What do you mean by it? Put your gloves on at once."

"I forgot to bring them," said Tistou.

"Very well, then, let's go on with our lesson. What is it that is required to control poverty and its deplorable consequences—let's think a little—something beginning with o——"

"I know," said Tistou, "oceans of money."

"Certainly not," said Mr. Turnbull, "it's *order* that's required."

Tistou was silent for a moment. He appeared

unconvinced. And when he had gathered his thoughts, he said, "Are you quite sure that this order you talk about really exists, Mr. Turnbull? I don't think it does."

Mr. Turnbull's ears turned so red that they no longer looked like ears at all, but tomatoes.

"Because if order did exist," said Tistou in a firm voice, "there wouldn't be any poverty."

The report Tistou got that day was far from good. Mr. Turnbull wrote in the notebook: "Inattentive and inclined to be argumentative. His generous feelings are uncurbed by a sense of realities."

But the following day—you've already guessed it —the following day, the Mirepoil newspapers announced a positive deluge of morning-glories. Moustache's advice had been followed to the letter.

Arches of sky-blue veiled the ugliness of the hovels, borders of geraniums lined the lawn-covered streets. This underprivileged district, which people avoided because it was so horrible to look at, had become the most beautiful in the whole town. Now they went to visit it as if it were a museum.

Its inhabitants decided to make a profit out of it. They put up a turnstile at the entrance and made people pay to come in. And there was work too: gardeners were needed and guides, sellers of picture post-cards and photographers. It was wealth.

In order to put this wealth to good use, it was decided to build among the trees a huge block containing nine hundred and ninety-nine beautiful apartments, each with a modern electric kitchen, in which all the inhabitants of the hovels might henceforth live in comfort. And as a lot of people were needed to build it, the unemployed found work.

At the first opportunity, Moustache congratulated Tistou.

"Oh, so there you are! You've made a first-class job of the slums! But the district is a little lacking in scent. Next time, give a thought to jasmine. It's a quick climber and it smells good."

Tistou promised Moustache to do better next time.

CHAPTER ELEVEN

In which TISTOU
decides to help Dr. Ayling

Tistou

made the acquaintance of the little sick girl when he visited the hospital.

The Mirepoil hospital, thanks to Mr. Father's generosity, was a very fine hospital, very large and very clean, and was provided with everything that could possibly be needed for curing every kind of illness. The sun shone in through the huge windows; the walls were white and bright. Tistou did not think the hospital at all ugly. And yet he felt—how can one express it?—he felt that there was something sad about it.

Dr. Ayling, who was in charge of the hospital, was a very learned, very kind man. You could see that at a glance. Tistou thought that he was rather like Moustache, the gardener, but a Moustache with large tortoise-shell spectacles instead of whiskers. Tistou told him so.

"The resemblance," said Dr. Ayling, "is no doubt due to the fact that Moustache and I are both concerned with tending life. Moustache tends the lives of plants and I tend the lives of human beings."

But tending the lives of human beings was much more difficult. Tistou quickly began to realize this as he listened to Dr. Ayling. To be a doctor was to wage continuous war. On the one hand there was disease always ready to slip into people's bodies, and on the other good health always ready to slip out. And then, there were thousands of kinds of disease and only one kind of good health. Disease wore all kinds of disguises in order not to be recognized. It had to be unmasked, discouraged, chased away, while good health had to be tempted to return, then held tight and prevented from running off.

"Have you ever been ill, Tistou?" asked Dr. Ayling.

"No, never."

"Really?"

But, indeed, the Doctor remembered that he had never been called to see Tistou. Mrs. Mother often suffered from headaches; Mr. Father sometimes had indigestion. Carolus, the manservant, had had bronchitis last winter. Tistou, nothing. From the day he was born the boy had been completely healthy; no measles, no chickenpox, not even a common cold. A very rare instance of continuous good health, a most exceptional one.

Dr. Ayling showed Tistou the room in which little pink lozenges were made up for coughs, yellow ointment for spots, and white powder for fever. He showed him the room in which you can see through people's bodies, like looking through a window, in order to discover where disease is lurking. And he showed him the room with mirrors in the ceiling where appendicitis and so many other things that threaten people's lives are cured.

"Since this is a place where evil is prevented, everything ought to be gay and happy," Tistou thought. "Where's this sadness I feel hidden?"

The Doctor opened the door of the room in which the little sick girl was lying.

"I'll leave you, Tistou. You can come and find me later in my office," said Dr. Ayling.

Tistou went into the room.

"How do you do?" he said to the little girl.

He thought she was very pretty, but very pale. Her dark hair curled about the pillow. She was about Tistou's age.

"How do you do?" she replied politely, but without moving her head. She was staring at the ceiling.

Tistou sat down beside her bed, his white hat on his knee.

"Dr. Ayling tells me that your legs won't walk. Are they better since you've been here?"

"No," said the little girl as politely as before; "but it doesn't matter."

"Why not?" asked Tistou.

"Because I've nowhere to go."

"I've got a garden," said Tistou, in order to say something.

"You're lucky. If I had a garden, I might want to get well in order to walk in it."

Tistou immediately looked at his thumbs. "If that's all she needs to make her happy . . ." he thought.

"Are you terribly bored?" he asked.

"Not terribly. I look at the ceiling and count the little cracks in it."

"Flowers would be better," thought Tistou. And, silently, he began to call: "Poppy, poppy . . . buttercup . . . daisy . . . jonquil!"

No doubt, the seeds flew in through the window, unless, of course, Tistou had brought them in on the soles of his shoes.

"At least, you're not unhappy?" he said.

"To know that you're unhappy, you've got to have been happy," said the little girl. "I was born ill."

Tistou realized that the sadness of the hospital lay in this room, inhabited the little girl's head. It made him feel sad too.

"Do people come to see you?"

"Oh, yes! In the morning, before breakfast, Nurse Thermometer comes. Then Dr. Ayling comes; he's very kind. He always talks very gently and gives me a caramel. At lunchtime it's Nurse Pill's turn, and at teatime Nurse Injections-that-hurt. And then comes a gentleman dressed in white who pretends that my legs are better. He ties strings to them to make them move. They all say that I'm going to get well. But I just look at the ceiling; it, at least, doesn't tell me lies."

While she was talking, Tistou had got to his feet and was busying himself about the bed.

"There's no doubt," thought Tistou, "that if this little girl's going to get well, she must have something to look forward to from day to day. Flowers, with the way they unfold and the surprises they spring on you, will most certainly be a help to her. A growing flower asks a fresh riddle every morning. One day it half-opens a bud, the next it uncurls a leaf as green as a frog, then it unfolds a petal. . . . In her eagerness for each day's surprise, perhaps the little girl will forget her illness. . . ."

Tistou's thumbs continued to be busy.

"I think you're going to get well," he said.

"What, you think so too?"

"Oh, yes, I'm sure of it. Good-by."

"Good-by," the little girl replied politely. "You are lucky to have a garden."

Dr. Ayling was awaiting Tistou seated behind his big chromium desk, which was covered with huge books.

"Well, Tistou," he asked, "what have you learned today? What do you know about medicine?"

"I've learned," said Tistou, "that medicine can't do much where there's a sad heart. I've learned that in order to get well one must want to live. Doctor, aren't there any pills for giving people hope?"

Dr. Ayling was astonished to discover so much wisdom in so small a boy.

"You've found out for yourself," he said, "the first thing a doctor must know."

"And the second, Doctor?"

"Is that to be a good doctor you must love your fellow men."

He gave Tistou a handful of caramels and wrote a good report in his notebook.

But Dr. Ayling was a good deal more astonished

the next morning, when he went into the little girl's room.

She was smiling. It was as if she had waked up in a meadow.

Narcissi were growing round her bedside table; the bedspread had become a coverlet of periwinkles; wild oats waved across the carpet. And then the flower, the flower to which Tistou had given all his care, a wonderful rose, continually changing as it unfurled a leaf or a bud, had entwined itself about the headboard and climbed up to the pillow. The little girl was no longer gazing at the ceiling; she was looking at the rose.

The rose leaned down on its long stalk to kiss her. It was the first time the little girl had ever been kissed.

That very evening her legs began to move. She liked life now.

CHAPTER TWELVE

In which the name of MIREPOIL
becomes longer

Y₀ᵤ may think
that the grown-ups were beginning to suspect something; that they were saying to themselves with simple
logic: "The mysterious flowers always appear in places
Tistou has been to the day before. It must therefore be
Tistou; let's watch him."

But if you think this because you know that Tistou
had green thumbs, grown-ups, as I've already told
you, have ready-made ideas, and hardly ever believe
that anything can exist that they don't already know.

From time to time someone comes along who
reveals some portion of the unknown; people always

laugh in his face to begin with; sometimes he's even thrown into prison because he's upset Mr. Turnbull's order; and then, when he's dead, and people see that he was right after all, they erect a statue to him. He's what is called a genius.

But that particular year there was no genius at Mirepoil to explain the inexplicable. And the Town Council were in a terrible state.

The Town Council is rather like the town's housekeeper. It has to see to the cleanliness of the sidewalks, indicate where the children may play and the beggars may beg, and where the buses must be parked at night. There must be no disorder; above all, no disorder.

But disorder had come to Mirepoil. It was no longer possible to be sure, from one day to the next, where there would be a street or a garden. Flowers climbed up the prison walls, concealed the slums, sprouted inside the hospital! If a Council were to submit to such fantastic things as these, a town would cease to be a town. One fine morning the Cathedral would decide to change its site in order to get a breath of fresh air, or perhaps even take to the river to cool off a little. . . .

"No, no; and again, no!" shouted the Town Councillors of Mirepoil, when summoned to an extraordinary meeting.

They were already talking of pulling up all the flowers.

Mr. Father intervened. And Mr. Father was much respected on the Council. Once again, he showed himself to be a man of quick and bold decision.

"Gentlemen," he said, "you are wrong to be angry. Moreover, it is always dangerous to be angry with things you don't understand. Not one of us knows the cause of these sudden flowerings. Pull up the flowers?

You cannot tell where they may grow again tomorrow. What's more, you must admit that these flowers are doing us more good than harm. The prisoners are no longer trying to escape. The slums have prospered. All the children in the hospital are getting well. Why be angry? Let's play up the flowers, and keep abreast of events rather than lag behind them."

"Yes, yes; and again, yes!" shouted the Councillors. "But how shall we set about it?"

Mr. Father went on with his speech.

"I put forward a somewhat daring suggestion. We must change the name of our town and call it from now on Mirepoil-les-Fleurs. With a name like that, no one ought to be surprised if flowers grow all over the place. And should the church steeple turn into a bunch of lilac tomorrow, everyone will think that this embellishment is merely part of our long-term policy."

"Hurrah, hurrah, hurrah!" cried the Councillors, giving Mr. Father their unanimous approval.

So the next day, since they had to take quick action, the Town Councillors in a body, preceded by the choir, an orphanage accompanied by two priests in their surplices, a delegation of grandfathers representing wisdom, Dr. Ayling representing science, a magistrate representing the law, two schoolmasters representing letters and a soldier in uniform on leave-pass representing the army, formed an imposing procession. They marched all the way to the station. There, to the cheers of a happy crowd, they unveiled a new placard on which was written in letters of gold:

MIREPOIL-LES-FLEURS

MIREPOIL-OF-THE-FLOWERS

It was a great day!

CHAPTER THIRTEEN

*In which an attempt
is made
to divert* TISTOU

MRS. MOTHER
was even more anxious than the Town Councillors,
but for other reasons. Her Tistou was no longer the
same boy.

The system of education invented by Mr. Father
had made him strangely serious; he was silent for
whole hours together.

"What are you thinking, Tistou?" asked Mrs.
Mother.

Tistou replied, "I'm just thinking that the world
could be so much better than it is."

Mrs. Mother frowned.

"Those are not thoughts suitable to your age, Tistou. Go and play with Gymnast."

"Gymnast thinks as I do," said Tistou.

Mrs. Mother became quite cross.

"This is really too much!" she said. "Are children to take their opinions from ponies these days?"

She spoke about it to Mr. Father, who thought that Tistou was in need of diversion.

"The pony, the pony," he said, "that's all very well, but he mustn't always be seeing the same animals. Let's send him to visit the Zoo."

But there, too, Tistou was unpleasantly surprised.

He had imagined the Zoo to be a fairy-tale place in which animals took delight in showing themselves off to the admiration of the visitors, a sort of paradise of beasts in which the boa constrictor did physical culture about the giraffe's legs, and the kangaroo put a baby bear in his pocket to take him out for a walk. He thought the jaguars, buffaloes, rhinoceroses, tapirs, lyre-birds, parrots and monkeys had a wonderful time among all kinds of exotic flowers and trees, just as they do in the picture-books.

Instead, he found that the Zoo was a place of cages in which mangy lions slept sadly by their empty feeding-troughs, where tigers were confined with tigers and monkeys with monkeys. He tried to comfort a panther which was walking up and down, up and down behind its bars. He wanted to give it a cooky. A keeper stopped him.

"It's forbidden, young man; stand back. These are dangerous animals," cried the keeper angrily.

"Where do they come from?" asked Tistou.

"From very far away. From Africa and Asia, how should I know?"

"Did anyone ask their permission to bring them here?"

The keeper shrugged his shoulders and went off, grumbling that he wasn't there to be made fun of.

But, for his part, Tistou was thinking. In the first place, he thought that the keeper ought not to be engaged in his calling at all, since he did not like the animals he had to look after. He also thought the animals must have brought some seeds from their own countries in their fur, and must have spread them about. . . .

It did not occur to any of the keepers in the Zoo to stop a little boy placing his thumbs in the earth before each cage. The keepers only thought that that particular little boy liked playing in the dirt.

And that was how it came about that, a few days later, an enormous baobab tree had grown in the lion's cage, that the monkeys were swinging from liana to liana, and water-lilies were in full flower in the crocodile's tank. The bear had his pine tree, the kangaroo his savanna; the herons and the rose-colored flamingoes stalked among reeds; and the multi-colored birds sang among giant jasmines. The Zoo of Mirepoil had become the most beautiful in the world, and the Town Councillors hastened to inform the Tourist Agencies of the fact.

"So now you're even working with tropical vegetation, are you?" said Moustache when he next saw Tistou. "That's very good indeed."

"It's really the best I could do for those poor wild animals, who were so bored far away from their homes," Tistou replied.

That week, the wild animals did not eat a single keeper.

CHAPTER FOURTEEN

In which TISTOU
asks some new questions
about War

IT sometimes happens that,
when grown-ups raise their voices, little boys do not
listen.

"Do you hear what I'm saying, Tistou?"

And Tistou would nod his head, saying, "Yes,
yes," in order to seem obedient, though he had not
heard a single word.

But as soon as grown-ups lower their voices and
start talking secrets, little boys at once listen as hard as
they can and try to understand what was not meant for
their ears. All little boys are alike in this, and Tistou
was no exception.

For some days past, there had been a good deal of whispering in Mirepoil. There were secrets in the air, even in the very carpets of the Shining House.

Mr. Father and Mrs. Mother sighed deeply as they read the newspapers. Carolus, the manservant, and Mrs. Amelia, the cook, gossiped in undertones at the washing-machine. Even Mr. Turnbull seemed to have lost his trumpeting voice.

Tistou caught words of ill-omen on the wing.

"Tension . . ." said Mr. Father, his voice grave.

"Crisis . . ." replied Mrs. Mother.

"Worsening . . ." added Mr. Turnbull.

Tistou thought that they were talking of illness; he was very concerned and went off, his thumbs at the ready, to find out which member of the household could be ill.

A turn in the garden proved to him that he was wrong: Moustache was in perfect health, the thorough-bred roans were frisking in the field, Gymnast showed every sign of being in perfect condition.

But the next day another word was on everyone's lips.

"War . . . it was inevitable," said Mr. Father.

"War . . . poor people!" said Mrs. Mother, sorrowfully shaking her head.

"War . . . and there we are! Just another one," said Mr. Turnbull. "It only remains to be seen who'll win."

"War . . . how terrible! Shall we never be done with it?" groaned Mrs. Amelia, on the point of tears.

"War . . . war . . . always wars," repeated Carolus, the manservant.

Tistou thought of war as something improper since people spoke about it with lowered voices, as something ugly, a grown-up disease worse than drunkenness, crueller than poverty, more dangerous than crime. Mr. Turnbull had already mentioned war to him and shown him the Mirepoil War Memorial. But since Mr. Turnbull had spoken rather loudly, Tistou had not properly understood him.

Tistou was not afraid. There was nothing of the coward about the boy; in certain respects he might indeed have been thought rash. You have already seen how he used to slide down the banisters. When he went to the river to bathe, he had to be stopped diving off the champion's high dive ten times in succession.

He would take a run and launch himself into the air, his arms widespread, in a swallow-dive. He would climb trees like nobody's business, going right to the topmost branches to pick the cherries no one else could reach. He never turned giddy. No, indeed, Tistou was far from timid.

But his idea of war had nothing to do with courage or fear. He merely found the idea intolerable, that was all.

He wanted information. Was war really as horrible as he imagined it to be? Obviously, the first person to consult was Moustache.

"I hope I'm not interrupting you, Mr. Moustache," he said to the gardener, who was clipping a hedge.

Moustache put down his shears.

"Not at all, not at all, my boy."

"Mr. Moustache, tell me, what do you think about war?"

The gardener looked surprised.

"I'm against it," he replied, tugging at his whiskers.

"Why are you against it?"

"Because . . . because even a little, unimportant war can annihilate a very big garden."

"Annihilate, what does that mean?"

"It means destroy, abolish, reduce to dust."

"Really? And have you actually seen gardens . . . annihilated by war, Mr. Moustache?" asked Tistou.

It seemed barely credible. But the gardener was not joking. He stood with bent head, his thick white eyebrows contracted in a frown, twisting his moustache in his fingers.

"Yes, yes, I've seen it happen," he replied. "I've seen a garden full of flowers die in two minutes. I saw the greenhouses smashed into a thousand pieces. So many bombs fell in that garden that it was no use ever thinking of cultivating it again. Even the earth was dead."

Tistou felt his throat contract.

"And whose garden was it?" he asked.

"It was mine," said Moustache, turning away to hide his grief, and picking up his shears.

Tistou was silent for a moment. He was thinking. He was trying to imagine the garden about him destroyed as that other garden had been, the greenhouses broken and the earth barren of flowers. Tears came to his eyes.

"Well, I shall go and tell everyone about it!" he cried. "Everyone must know. I shall tell Amelia and I shall tell Carolus. . . ."

"Oh, Carolus is worse off than I am. He lost his country."

"His country? He lost his country in a war? How is that possible?"

"Well, it's what happened. His country has completely disappeared. He could never find it again. That's why he's here."

"I was quite right in thinking that war is a horrible thing, if you can lose your country in it as you lose a handkerchief," Tistou thought.

"There's even worse than that," Moustache added. "You mentioned Amelia, the cook. Well, Amelia lost her son. Others have lost arms or legs, or their heads even. Everyone loses something in a war."

It occurred to Tistou that war was the greatest and most horrible disorder that could happen in the world since everyone lost in it what they loved best.

"What can be done to prevent its happening? . . ." he wondered. "Mr. Turnbull must be against war, since he hates disorder so much. I shall talk to him about it tomorrow."

CHAPTER FIFTEEN

In which TISTOU *has a lesson*
in Geography, followed by
a lesson on Business,
and in which the conflict
between the Go-its
and the Get-outs spreads
in an unforeseen manner

MR. TURNBULL
was sitting behind his desk. He had recovered his
trumpet-like voice and was shouting into three telephones at the same time. It was clear that Mr. Turnbull
was a very busy man.

"It's always the same when a war breaks out
somewhere in the world," he said to Tistou. "Our
work at Mirepoil is doubled at once."

And, indeed, Tistou had noticed that morning that the factory siren had blown for twice the usual length of time and that twice the usual number of workers had appeared. The nine chimneys were making so much smoke that the whole sky was darkened.

"I'll come back when you're not so busy," said Tistou.

"What did you want to ask me?"

"I wanted to know where this war has broken out."

Mr. Turnbull rose to his feet and led Tistou to an enormous globe of the world. He turned it round and placed his finger on the center of it.

"Do you see this desert?" he asked. "Well, it's there."

Under Mr. Turnbull's finger Tistou saw a pink, almond-shaped expanse.

"Why has the war happened there, Mr. Turnbull?"

"It's not very difficult to understand."

When Mr. Turnbull said something was not very difficult to understand, Tistou's heart sank; it was generally very complicated indeed. But this time Tistou was determined to listen attentively.

"Not at all difficult," repeated Mr. Turnbull. "This desert belongs to nobody. . . ."

"To nobody," Tistou repeated to himself.

". . . but on the right is the country of the Go-its, and on the left the country of the Get-outs."

"Go-its . . . Get-outs. . . ." Tistou repeated to himself once more; he was really being very attentive.

". . . Well, some time ago the Go-its announced that they wanted this desert; the Get-outs replied that they wanted it too. The Go-its sent a telegram to the Get-outs telling them to go away. The Get-outs replied by radio that they forbade the Go-its to remain in occupation; so now their armies are on the march and when they meet there'll be a battle."

"What is there in that pink sugar almond . . . I mean in that desert?"

"Nothing at all. Stones. . . ."

"So they're just going to fight for stones?"

"They want to own what's underneath."

"What's under the desert?"

"Oil."

"What do they want oil for?"

"They want it so that the other can't have it. They want oil, because oil's an essential material for making war."

Tistou had known that Mr. Turnbull's explanations would become very difficult to understand.

He shut his eyes in order to think better.

"If I've understood properly, the Go-its and the Get-outs are going to fight a war for oil because oil is an essential material for fighting wars." He reopened his eyes.

"Well, it's stupid," he said.

Mr. Turnbull's ears turned scarlet.

"Do you want to get zero for your lesson, Tistou?"

"No," replied Tistou, "but what I do want is that the Go-its and the Get-outs should not fight."

This proof of goodheartedness for the moment lessened Mr. Turnbull's anger.

"Of course, of course," he said, shrugging his shoulders. "No one wants war, ever. But it has always existed. . . ."

"What can I do?" wondered Tistou. "Put my thumbs on the pink almond?"

"Is the desert far away?" he asked.

"Half-way between here and the other side of the world."

"So the war can't spread as far as Mirepoil?"

"It's not impossible. Once a war's begun, one can never tell where it will end. The Go-its may call a Great Power to their assistance, the Get-outs ask help of another. And the two Great Powers will fight. It's called an extension of the conflict."

Tistou's head was positively buzzing. "Yes," he said to himself. "War's really like some appalling sort of crab-grass growing on the face of the globe. What plants can I use to fight it with?"

"We'll now go to the factory," said Mr. Turnbull. "You'll see it working to capacity; it'll be an instructive lesson for you."

He shouted some orders into his three telephones and then accompanied Tistou downstairs.

Tistou was at first deafened by the noise. The steam-hammers were banging away with all their might, the machines were humming like a million spinning-tops, chains were clanging; one had to shout

to make oneself heard, even with a voice like Mr. Turnbull's.

Tistou was blinded by the fountains of sparks rising on all sides; molten steel gushing down to the floor like huge burning brooks; the heat was appalling, the workmen seemed small and black against the huge background of the factory.

After the foundry, Tistou visited the burnishing, turning and fitting departments, the departments where rifles, machine guns, tanks and trucks were made, for Mr. Father's factory made everything required for making war in the way of arms and munitions.

The following day was the day for shipping and the armaments were being packed with as much care as if they had been china.

Finally, Mr. Turnbull showed Tistou two huge guns, as long as cathedral spires. They were as bright and gleaming as if they had been covered with butter.

Suspended on chains, the guns moved slowly through the air; then they were lowered gently, gently, on to trailer-trucks which were so long you couldn't see the end of them.

"Those are the guns which have brought wealth to Mirepoil, Tistou," said Mr. Turnbull proudly. "With every shell they fire they can destroy four homes as big as yours."

This information did not appear to impress Tistou with a similar pride.

"So," he thought, "each time one of these guns fires, there'll be four Tistous without a home, four Caroluses without a staircase, and four Amelias without a kitchen. . . . Those must be the things by which people lose their gardens, their countries, their legs or members of their families. . . . Well, really!"

And the hammers were pounding and the furnaces glowing white hot.

"Whose side are you on, Mr. Turnbull?" Tistou asked, shouting at the top of his voice because of the appalling din.

"What's that?"

"I said: Whose side are you on in this war?"

"Oh, the Go-its," Mr. Turnbull shouted back.

"And my father?"

"He is, too."

"Why?"

"Because they've been our loyal friends for a long while."

"Of course," thought Tistou, "if one's friends are attacked it's quite right to help them defend themselves."

"So those guns are going to the Go-its?" he went on.

"Only the one on the right," shouted Mr. Turnbull. "The other's for the Get-outs."

"How do you mean, for the Get-outs?" cried Tistou indignantly.

"Because they're good customers, too."

So one gun from Mirepoil would be firing against another gun from Mirepoil, and a garden would be destroyed on each side!

"That's business," Mr. Turnbull added.

"Well, I think your business is horrible!"

"What's that?" asked Mr. Turnbull, lowering his head because the noise of the steam-hammers drowned Tistou's voice.

"I said that your business is horrible, because . . ."

A terrific box on the ear stopped him short. The

conflict between the Go-its and the Get-outs had been suddenly extended to Tistou's ear.

"That's what war's like! You ask for an explanation, you give your opinion—and what happens? You get a box on the ear! Supposing I made some holly

grow in your trousers, what would you say then?" thought Tistou, as he gazed at Mr. Turnbull with his eyes full of tears. "That's it, holly in his trousers, or perhaps thistles . . . !"

He clasped his fingers together. . . . And it was then that the idea, the great idea, came to him.

The business lesson, as you can well imagine, came to an end there. Tistou got two zeros, and Mr. Turnbull reported him at once to Mr. Father. The latter was extremely disappointed. His Tistou, who was one day to succeed him and become the master of Mirepoil, was really showing very little talent for controlling so splendid a business.

"I shall really have to talk to him very seriously," said Mr. Father. "Where is he?"

"He's gone to take refuge with the gardener, as usual," replied Mr. Turnbull.

"Very well, we'll see about that later. At the moment we must finish the packing."

Because of the urgent orders, the factory was working without stopping. All night long, the nine chimneys wore great, red, glowing crowns.

But, that night, Mr. Father, who had not even taken time off to dine and was watching the work of the departments from a little glass tower, was pleasantly surprised. Tistou had returned to the factory and was walking slowly along the line of packing-cases containing rifles, then he climbed into the trucks, leaned over the engines and slipped in among the big guns.

"Well done, Tistou," Mr. Father said to himself. "The boy's trying to make up for his double zero. Spendid! There's still some hope for him!"

And, indeed, Tistou had never appeared so serious and so busy before! His hair was standing straight up on end. He was continually putting his hand in his pocket and pulling out little pieces of paper.

"It even looks as if he were taking notes," thought Mr. Father. "I hope he doesn't pinch his fingers among those machine guns. He's a good boy when all's said and done, and quick to see when he's at fault."

There were surprises in store for Mr. Father.

CHAPTER SIXTEEN

*In which
surprising pieces of news
follow hard upon each other*

EVERYONE knows

that newspapers always talk of war in capital letters. These letters are kept in a special tray. And it was precisely before this capital-letter-tray that the editor of the *Mirepoil Star*, a well-known daily newspaper, was standing in some hesitation.

The editor kept turning about, sighing and wiping his forehead, which is always a sign of emotion and perplexity. The man was most disturbed.

Sometimes he took out a big capital letter, the kind that is kept for important victories; but immediately put it back again. Sometimes he took out a medium-sized capital letter, the kind that is kept for wars which are not going very well, for campaigns which show no signs of coming to an end, or for unexpected retreats. But this size of capital letter would not do either; he put it back in the cupboard.

At one moment he seemed to have made up his mind to use very small capital letters, the kind that are used for announcements which put everyone in a bad temper, like SUGAR SHORTAGE or NEW TAX ON JAM. But these would not do either. And the editor of the *Mirepoil Star* sighed all the more. He was really very disturbed indeed.

He had to tell the inhabitants of Mirepoil, his faithful readers, a piece of news that was so unexpected, and so serious in its consequences, that he did not know how to set about it. The war between the Go-its and the Get-outs had come to an end. And how was one to admit to the public that a war could just stop like that, without a winning or a losing side, without an international conference, without anything at all?

The poor editor would have loved to have been able to print right along the top of his first page some sensational headline such as LIGHTNING GO-IT ADVANCE or HEAVY GET-OUT OFFENSIVE.

But this was out of the question. The reports from the pink almond on the map were definite: the war had not taken place and the reason for its failure to do so cast doubts upon the quality of the arms delivered by the Mirepoil factory, upon Mr. Father's technical competence and upon that of his workshops and workpeople.

In fact, a disaster had occurred.

Let us try, with the editor of the *Mirepoil Star*, to reconstruct these tragic events.

Climbing, romping, clinging plants had taken root in the cases of arms! How had they got there? Why? No one could explain.

Ivy, briony, bindweed, ampelopsis, knot-grass and dodder had formed an inextricable skein, matted with the glue of the black henbane about the machine guns, submachine guns and revolvers.

Neither the Go-its nor the Get-outs had been able to unpack their cases.

The correspondents, in their despatches, emphasized the particularly harmful qualities of burdock,

which had fastened itself by means of the little hooks upon its burrs to the bayonets. What could be done with rifles that flowered, with bayonets that you couldn't poke and whose efficiency was completely

destroyed by pretty bunches of flowers? They had to be thrown away.

Equally useless were the magnificent trucks, which had been so carefully camouflaged with gray and yellow lines! Brambles, goose-grass and several varieties of nettles, the stinging variety in particular, were growing in abundance upon their seats. The drivers all got nettle rash, and were thus the only casualties in the war. White-coated nurses made these soldiers, whose cruel itchings prevented them from sitting down, lie still while they applied warm compresses.

And here must be recorded a really pitiful incident caused by balsam. That a modest wild flower should be able to create a panic among soldiers is perfectly comprehensible if you know that balsam has pods which explode at the slightest touch.

The engines were all full of it. Balsam swarmed in the carburetors of the armored cars, in the tanks of the motorcycles. At the first contact of the self-starter, at the first kick at the starting pedal, there was a growing, spreading sound of dull explosions which, if they did

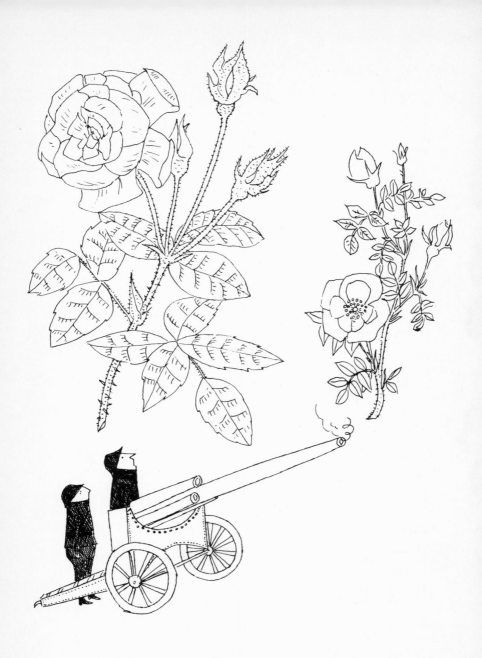

no harm, nevertheless had a shattering effect on the morale of the troops.

What of the tanks? Their turrets were blocked up. Eglantine mingled with gorse and herb-bennet enclosed their mechanism in a mass of roots, clusters, stalks and thorny branches. The tanks were also, therefore, useless.

A rain of foxgloves, bluebells and cornflowers had fallen on the Go-its' positions and they had replied, flooding the Get-outs with buttercups, daisies and roses. A general had had his cap knocked off by a bunch of violets!

Countries are not taken with roses, and battles of flowers have never been looked on as very serious engagements.

Peace between the Go-its and the Get-outs was concluded on the spot. The armies retired and the desert, a pink sugar almond, was left to the sky, to solitude and to freedom.

CHAPTER SEVENTEEN

In which TISTOU
bravely owns up

THE mere fact of silence itself
sometimes wakes you up. That morning, Tistou
jumped out of bed because the big factory siren failed
to sound. He went to the window. The Mirepoil
factory was not working; the nine chimneys were no
longer smoking.

Tistou ran out into the garden. Moustache was
sitting on his barrow and reading the newspaper, a
very rare event.

"Ah, there you are!" he cried. "We must praise
good work when we see it. I'd never have thought
you'd be as successful as that!"

Moustache was positively beaming with delight. He kissed Tistou, or rather enveloped his head in his moustache.

And then, with that slightly melancholy air which men have when they've finished their task, he added:

"There's nothing more I can teach you. You now know as much as I do and you work much faster."

Coming from such a master as Moustache, the compliment warmed Tistou's heart.

By the stables, Tistou found Gymnast.

"It's wonderful," Tistou whispered into his soft, brown ear. "I've stopped a war with flowers."

The pony did not appear at all surprised.

"By the way," he said in reply, "a bundle of white clover would not be unwelcome. It's my favorite breakfast dish; and there seems to be less and less of it in the field. Try to remember about it some time."

Tistou heard these words with amazement. Not because the pony was talking—he'd known about that

for a long time—but because Gymnast knew that he had green thumbs.

"It's lucky Gymnast never talks to anyone but me," Tistou said to himself.

And he went thoughtfully up to the house. Clearly, the pony knew a great deal.

In the Shining House things were not going quite as they usually did. In the first place, and it's a fact, the windows were not as bright. Amelia was not singing over her stove: "Nina, Nina, what have you done with your life . . ." which was her favorite song. Carolus, the manservant, was not polishing the banisters.

Mrs. Mother had left her room at eight o'clock, which she usually only did when she was going on a journey. She was having breakfast in the dining-room; or rather her breakfast stood untouched before her. She hardly noticed Tistou come into the room.

Mr. Father had not gone to his office. He was in the big drawing-room with Mr. Turnbull, and they were both pacing to and fro in such an agitated state that sometimes they banged into each other, and at others turned their backs on each other. Their conversation sounded like a thunderstorm.

"Ruin! Dishonor! Bankruptcy! Unemployment!" shouted Mr. Father.

And Mr. Turnbull replied like an echo of the thunder sounding among the clouds, "Conspiracy! Sabotage! A pacifist plot!"

"Oh, my guns, my beautiful guns!" went on Mr. Father.

Tistou, standing on the threshold of the half-open door dared not interrupt them.

"That's what grown-up people are like," he said to himself. "Mr. Turnbull assured me that everyone was against war, but that it was an inevitable evil, and that there was nothing to be done about it. I manage to stop a war and they might be pleased, but they're not; they get angry instead."

And Mr. Father cried, beside himself, as he bumped into Mr. Turnbull, "Oh, if I could only find the wretch who sowed flowers among my guns!"

"Oh, if I could lay my hands on him!" agreed Mr. Turnbull, turning his back on Mr. Father. "But perhaps no one is actually responsible. . . . Some superhuman agency . . ."

"There must be an inquiry. . . . It's high treason."

Tistou, as you know, was a brave boy. He opened the door and advanced across the flowered carpet till he was standing right under the great crystal chandelier, opposite the portrait of Mr. Grandfather. He drew a deep breath.

"I sowed the flowers among the guns," he said.

And then he shut his eyes, expecting a box on the ear. As it did not come, he opened them again.

Mr. Father had come to a halt at one end of the drawing-room and Mr. Turnbull at the other. They looked at Tistou, but somehow as if they were not seeing him. It was as if they had neither heard nor understood what he had said.

"They don't believe me," thought Tistou. To add weight to the confession, he enumerated his other triumphs, rather as if he were giving the solution to a charade.

"The morning-glories in the slums, that was me! The prison was me! The coverlet of periwinkles for the little sick girl was me! And the baobab tree in the lion's cage was me, too!"

Mr. Father and Mr. Turnbull went on staring like statues. The idea of Tistou as a sort of constructional

florist had clearly not penetrated their minds. They looked exactly like people who were on the point of saying, "Stop talking nonsense and don't interrupt your elders and betters."

"They think I'm boasting," thought Tistou. "I must prove to them that it's true."

He went up to the portrait of Mr. Grandfather and placed his two thumbs, keeping them there for several seconds, against the gun on which the venerable founder of the Mirepoil Armament Works was leaning.

The canvas quivered a little, and then from the gun's muzzle emerged a shoot of lily-of-the-valley, first one leaf then another, followed by its white bells.

"There!" said Tistou. "I've got green thumbs."

He expected Mr. Turnbull to grow purple in the face and Mr. Father to turn pale. But it was the opposite that happened.

Mr. Father collapsed into a chair, his face purple, while Mr. Turnbull, pale as potato, fell full-length upon the carpet.

From this double sign Tistou realized that making

flowers grow inside guns was apt gravely to upset the lives of grown-up people.

He left the room with his ear intact, which shows that courage always has its reward.

CHAPTER EIGHTEEN

*In which certain Grown-ups
at last give up
their Ready-made Ideas*

MR. FATHER,
as you will have gathered during the course of this
narrative, was a man of quick decisions.

All the same, it took him a good week to think the
situation over and face up to it.

Surrounded by his best engineers, he held a
number of board-meetings, in which Mr. Turnbull
took part. He shut himself up alone in his study and
spent long hours there with his head between his
hands. He made notes and tore them up again.

The situation amounted to this: Tistou had green
thumbs; he had used his green thumbs and, in doing
so, had brought the Mirepoil factory to a stop.

Because, of course, the Ministers for War and Commanders-in-Chief, who normally bought their armaments at Mirepoil, had at once cancelled their orders and withdrawn their trade.

"Might as well go to a florist!" they said.

There was, of course, one solution which occurred to unimaginative people: to shut Tistou up in prison because he upset the natural order of things, announce through the press that the disturber of the peace had been placed where he could do no more harm, replace the leafy guns with the latest models and send out a circular to all the generals informing them that the factory was in full production again.

But Mr. Turnbull—yes, Mr. Turnbull himself—opposed this solution.

"It's not so easy to recover from a set-back of this kind," he said, for once without shouting. "Our products will be viewed with suspicion for a long time to come. And to put Tistou in prison will do no one any good. He'd merely make oaks grow till their roots toppled the walls over, and then he'd escape. It's no good trying to oppose the forces of nature."

Mr. Turnbull had changed a lot! Ever since the day he had fallen in the drawing-room, his ears had been pale and his voice moderated. Besides—and why not admit it?—it pained Mr. Turnbull to think of Tistou wearing convict's clothes and walking round and round in a prison yard, even a flowery prison. Prison is one of those things one can contemplate calmly for people one does not know. But it's quite a different matter when a little boy one knows and is fond of is concerned. And this is something one had really not expected! Mr. Turnbull, in spite of his remonstrances, the zeros and the box on the ear, Mr. Turnbull, as soon as prison was mentioned, discovered that he was very fond of Tistou and would hate to be deprived of seeing him. Sometimes people who shout at you in loud voices are like that.

Besides, Mr. Father would not hear a word of putting Tistou in prison. I have already told you that Mr. Father was a kind man. He was a kind man and he was an armaments manufacturer. At first sight these things might appear incompatible. He adored his son and manufactured arms to make other people's children orphans. This is a more usual state of affairs than you might suppose.

"We have been successful in two things," he said to Mrs. Mother. "We made the best guns, and we made Tistou a happy child. It appears that those two things can no longer go together."

Mrs. Mother was sweet, kind and beautiful. An enchanting person. She always listened to her husband with the greatest interest and admiration. Since the unfortunate business of the Go-its' war, she had felt herself vaguely to blame, without quite knowing how. Mothers always feel somewhat to blame when their children upset the lives of grown-up people and run the risk of getting into trouble.

"What shall we do, my dear, what shall we do?" she replied.

"I'm as much concerned for the future of the factory as I am for Tistou's," continued Mr. Father. "We had preconceived ideas about the boy's future; we thought that he would succeed me as I succeeded my father. His path was mapped out for him: wealth, consideration. . . ."

"It was a ready-made idea," said Mrs. Mother.

"Yes, it was! A ready-made idea, and a very convenient one. Now we must have another. It's obvious that the boy has no taste for armaments."

"His vocation appears to be more towards agriculture." Mr. Father remembered Mr. Turnbull's resigned words: "It's no good trying to oppose the forces of nature. . . ."

"Clearly one can do nothing against those forces," thought Mr. Father, "but one can make use of them."

He rose to his feet, walked across the room, turned about and tugged at the points of his waistcoat.

"My dear wife," he said, "this is my decision."

"I am sure it will be an admirable one," said Mrs. Mother, her eyes dewy with tears, for, at that moment, Mr. Father's face wore a movingly heroic expression, while his hair shone more brightly than ever.

"We shall transform the gun factory," he declared, "into a flower factory."

Great men of business, of course, have a secret of making these sudden changes, these abrupt recoveries in the face of adversity.

The plan was immediately put in hand. Its success was electrifying.

The battle of the violets and buttercups had created a great stir in the world. Public opinion was prepared. All the preceding events, the mysterious flowerings, even the name of the town, Mirepoil-les-Fleurs, all these things assisted the development of the new business.

Mr. Turnbull, who was in charge of the publicity, had huge posters erected on all the roads of the neighborhood, saying:

PLANT THE FLOWERS

WHICH GROW

IN A SINGLE NIGHT

or:

MIREPOIL FLOWERS

EVEN GROW ON STEEL

But his best slogan was undoubtedly:

SAY NO TO WAR, BUT SAY IT
WITH FLOWERS

Orders poured in and prosperity returned to the Shining House.

Dites non à
la guerre mais
dites le
avec
des fleurs

CHAPTER NINETEEN

In which TISTOU
makes a Final Discovery

STORIES never end
when you think they are going to. You doubtless think
that everything there was to say has been said; you prob-
ably think you know Tistou pretty well. But one can
never know anyone completely. Even our best friends
can surprise us.

Indeed, Tistou was no longer concealing the fact
that he had green thumbs. On the contrary, the fact
was being much talked of, as Tistou had become
famous, not only in Mirepoil, but throughout the
whole world.

The factory was in full production. The nine chimneys were covered to their very tops with creepers and splendid flowers. The workshops were filled with the most delicious scents.

Flowered carpets were being manufactured for private houses, and flowered hangings to replace curtains and wallpaper. Whole gardens were being delivered by the truckload. Mr. Father had even received an order for camouflaging skyscrapers because the people who lived in them, so it was said, were often subject to a form of vertigo which drove them to throw themselves out of windows on the hundred-and-thirtieth floor. Living so far above the ground, they were naturally unlikely to feel altogether comfortable, and it was thought that flowers might make them feel less giddy.

Moustache had become chief technical adviser. Tistou worked hard at perfecting his art. He was now engaged in inventing new flowers. He had succeeded in making a blue rose. Every petal was like a chip of sky, and he had perfected several sun-colors: sunshine, dawn and sunset in a splendid crimson-gold.

When he had finished his work, he went to play in the garden with the little girl, who was now cured. Gymnast ate nothing now but white clover.

"So, you're happy now, are you?" asked Gymnast one day.

"Oh, yes, very happy," replied Tistou.

"You aren't bored?"

"Not at all."

"You don't want to leave us? You're going to stay with us?"

"Of course. Why do you ask such odd questions?"

"Just an idea I had."

"What do you mean? Aren't all my troubles over?" asked Tistou.

"We shall see . . . we shall see . . ." said the pony, going back to his clover.

A few mornings later, there was a piece of news that made everyone in the Shining House very sad. Moustache had failed to wake up.

"Moustache has decided to sleep for ever," Mrs. Mother explained to Tistou.

"Can I go and see him sleeping?"

"No. You can't see him any more. He's gone on a long, long journey. He won't ever come back."

Tistou found this very difficult to understand.

"People don't go on journeys," he thought, "with their eyes shut. If he's asleep, he might at least have said goodnight to me. And if he's gone away, he might have said good-by. There's something very odd about all this. They're hiding something from me."

He went to talk to Amelia, the cook.

"Poor Moustache is in the sky," said Amelia. "He's now happier than we are."

"If he's happy, why call him poor, and if he's poor, how can he be happy?" Tistou wondered.

Carolus had another version. According to him, Moustache was underground in the cemetery.

All this seemed very contradictory.

Underground or in the sky? This had to be cleared up. Moustache could not be everywhere at once.

Tistou went to find Gymnast.

"I know," said the pony. "Moustache is dead."

Gymnast always told the truth; it was one of his principles.

"Dead?" cried Tistou. "But there hasn't been a war, has there?"

"You don't need a war to die," replied the pony. "War is merely an extra sort of death. Moustache is dead because he was very old. Every life comes to an end."

For Tistou the sun seemed to lose its gold, the field turned dark, the very air stank. These are signs of a peculiar form of disquiet that grown-ups believe they alone can feel; but young people of Tistou's age know it too. It is called sorrow.

Tistou put his arms round the pony's neck and cried into his mane.

"Cry away, Tistou, cry away," said Gymnast. "It'll do you good. Grown-ups stop themselves crying; but they're wrong. Their tears become frozen inside them and that's what makes their hearts so hard."

But Tistou was a strange boy. He refused to submit to disaster so long as he had not put his thumbs to it. He dried his tears and tried to think things out.

"In the sky or underground?" he repeated to himself.

He decided to try the nearest place first. And the next day, after luncheon, he left the garden and ran all the way to the cemetery. It was full of trees and not sad at all.

"They're like black flames burning in the sunlight," he thought, gazing at the beautiful dark cypresses.

He came upon the gardener who, with his back turned towards him, was raking a path. He had a moment of wild hope. . . . But then the gardener turned round. He was just an ordinary cemetery

gardener, and did not look the least like the gardener for whom Tistou was searching.

"Can you tell me where Mr. Moustache is?" asked Tistou.

"Third row on the left," said the gardener, still busily raking.

"He must be here then . . ." thought Tistou.

Tistou walked on among the graves and stopped at the last, which was quite new.

On the gravestone was an inscription composed by the schoolmaster:

> Here lies Mr. Moustache,
> Whose work is done.
> He was the friend of flowers.
> Passers-by, shed a tear.

Then Tistou set to work. "Moustache won't be able to resist a fine peony. He'll want to talk to it," thought Tistou. He poked his thumbs into the ground and waited for a few seconds. The peony began to sprout from the earth, grew taller, blossomed, bowed its head, heavy as a cabbage, towards the inscription. But the gravestone never moved.

"Perhaps scented flowers will do the trick," thought Tistou. "He had a very sensitive nose." And he conjured up syringas, gardenias, jasmin, mimosa and tuberoses. Within a few minutes the grave was surrounded by a whole shrubbery. But it remained a grave.

"Perhaps a flower he didn't know would do it," Tistou said to himself. "However tired one is, curiosity can always wake one up."

But death laughs at enigmas. It is death that poses them.

For a whole hour Tistou gave rein to his imagination in order to produce a flower that had never been seen before. He invented a butterfly flower which had two pistils like antennae and two widespread petals which quivered at the least breath of wind. But it was without effect.

When at last he went away, his fingers dirty and his head held low, he left behind him the most astonishing grave that had ever been seen in a cemetery. But Moustache had not responded.

Tistou crossed the field to Gymnast.

"Do you know, Gymnast . . .?"

"Yes, I know," the pony replied. "You have discovered that death is the only sad thing that flowers can't keep from happening."

And as the pony was also a moralist, he added: "That's why men are very stupid to try to kill each other, as they're always doing."

Tistou looked up at the clouds and thought for a long time.

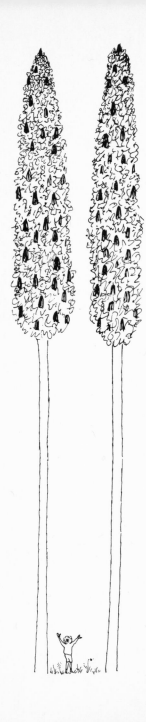

CHAPTER TWENTY

*In which, at last,
we find out
who* TISTOU *was*

IFor several days
he was busy with it; it took up all his time; indeed, he
could think of nothing else. And what was it? His
ladder.

"Tistou is making a ladder; quite a new departure
for him," the people were saying in Mirepoil.

No one knew more than that. What was the ladder
for? To what use was it to be put? Why a ladder rather
than a tower or a beflowered summer-house?

Tistou was rather evasive about it.

"I just want to make a ladder, that's all."

He had selected the site, right in the middle of the field.

Generally speaking, a ladder is carpenter's work. But Tistou was not using sawed wood.

He had begun by poking his thumbs deep into the earth and as far apart as he could stretch his arms.

"The ladder's roots must be sound," he explained to the pony, who was watching his labors with interest.

Two trees began to grow; two fine tall trees with close-knit branches. In under a week, they were ninety feet high. Faithful to Moustache's precepts, Tistou made them a little speech every day. This treatment produced the best possible results.

The trees were of a very original kind; their trunks had something of the elegance of an Italian poplar, but with the toughness of yew or box; their leaves were serrated like those of an oak, but they had vertical seed-pods like fir-cones.

But when the two had grown to over one-hundred-and-eighty feet, the serrated leaves gave place to bluish needles, then hairy buds appeared which caused Carolus to say that the trees belonged to a species well known in his country called bird-catcher's sorb.

"That, a sorb?" cried Amelia, the cook. "Haven't you noticed that they've got white, scented buds? They're acacias, I tell you, and I know what I'm talking about because I use the flowers when I make fritters."

But both Amelia and Carolus were neither wrong nor right. Everyone could see the species they liked most in these trees. They were trees without a name.

They were soon over three hundred feet high, and on misty days their tops were hidden.

But, you will say, two trees, however high they may be, have never made a ladder.

It was now, however, that the wistaria began to grow. A peculiar kind of wistaria, moreover, that appeared to have something of the hop vine about it. Indeed, it had one remarkable peculiarity: it grew in perfectly horizontal strands between the two trees. It gripped hard the trunk of one tree, jumped the intervening space, caught the trunk of the other, wrapped itself round it three times, tied a knot in its own stalk, climbed a little higher and jumped back to the trunk of the first tree. It thus formed the rungs of a ladder. When the wistaria all suddenly flowered at once, it was like a lavender waterfall pouring from the sky.

"If Moustache is really up there, as everyone says," Tistou confided to Gymnast, "he's certain to take advantage of the ladder to come down and see me, even if it's only for a moment."

"I think you're imagining things," the pony said.

"It makes me very unhappy not to see him . . . and not to know where he is," said Tistou.

The ladder continued to grow. It was photographed in color for the magazines, of which one wrote: "The ladder of flowers at Mirepoil is the eighth wonder of the world."

If its readers had been asked to name the other seven, they would have found some difficulty in doing so. You ask your parents and see!

But in spite of it all, Moustache did not climb down to earth.

"I'll wait for another three days," Tistou decided, "then I shall know what to do."

The third day came.

It was early in the morning. The moon was setting, the sun had not yet risen, and the stars were fading into sleep, when Tistou got out of bed. It was the moment of half-light between night and day.

Tistou was wearing a long white nightshirt.

"Where are my slippers?" he wondered. He found one under the bed and the other under the chest-of-drawers.

He slid down the banisters, crept out, and went to his ladder in the middle of the field. Gymnast was there too. His coat looked bedraggled, his ears were laid back and his mane unkempt.

"You're up very early," Tistou said.

"I didn't go to the stables last night," the pony explained. "I'm even prepared to admit that I've been trying to gnaw through your trees all night; but the wood is too hard. My teeth aren't strong enough."

"You mean you wanted to cut down my beautiful ladder?" cried Tistou. "Why? Was it to stop me climbing it?"

"Yes," said the pony.

There were pearls of dew on the grass. And in the pale light of dawn, Tistou saw two huge tears shining in the pony's eyes.

When horses cry, it's always for some important reason.

"Really, Gymnast, you mustn't cry so loudly, you'll wake everybody up," said Tistou. "What are you worried about? You know I never feel giddy. I'm only going up and coming down again; I must be back in the house before Carolus gets up. . . ."

But Gymnast went on crying.

"Oh, I knew. . . . I knew it was bound to happen . . ." he kept on saying.

"I'll try to bring you back a little star," said Tistou by way of consolation. "I'll see you again soon, Gymnast."

"Good-by," said the pony.

He watched Tistou jump on to the wistaria rungs and followed his climb with his eyes.

Tistou, light and agile, went steadily upwards. Soon his nightshirt looked no larger than a handkerchief.

Gymnast stretched his neck upwards. Tistou was growing smaller and smaller, soon he was no bigger than a marble, then a green pea, then a pin's head, then a grain of dust. When he had quite disappeared, Gymnast walked sadly away and began browsing on the grass in the field, though he was not at all hungry.

But Tistou could still see the ground from his ladder.

"How extraordinary," he thought, "the fields all look blue."

He stopped for a moment. At those heights everything changes in appearance. The Shining House still shone, but with the tiny glow of a diamond.

The wind romped in Tistou's nightshirt and bellied it out like a sail.

"I must hold on tight," he thought; and went on climbing. But instead of becoming more difficult, Tistou's climb became easier and easier, as he progressed.

The wind had fallen. Noise had faded into silence. The sun shone like a huge fire that did not burn. The earth was no more than a shadow, and then no more at all.

Tistou did not at once realize that the ladder had come to an end. He grasped the fact only when he became aware that he had lost his favorite slippers. There was no more ladder, and yet he was still rising, easily, effortlessly.

He was brushed by a huge white wing.

"How odd," he thought, "a wing without a bird."

And suddenly he was engulfed in an enormous white silky cloud, and could see nothing any more.

Then he heard a voice, a voice that sounded like Moustache's voice, but much louder and deeper. He heard it say, "So there you are!"

And he disappeared for ever into that mysterious world of which even people who write stories know nothing.

And yet, so that Mr. Father and Mrs. Mother and all the other people who loved him should not be anxious, Tistou left a last message through the agency of Gymnast. The pony, as I've told you, knew a great deal.

Hardly was Tistou out of sight, when the pony had begun grazing, though he was not hungry. But he browsed and browsed, as quickly as he could. And he browsed in a very odd way, as if he were making a special sort of design, or following a tracing which had been already marked out. And as he moved forward, the grass he ate was replaced by little golden flowers, which grew thick and close in its stead. When he had finished he went and took a rest.

When the inhabitants of the Shining House came out that morning and called Tistou all over the place, they found two little slippers in the middle of the field and this message written in beautiful golden flowers:

TISTOU ETAIT UN ANGE

TISTOU WAS AN ANGEL

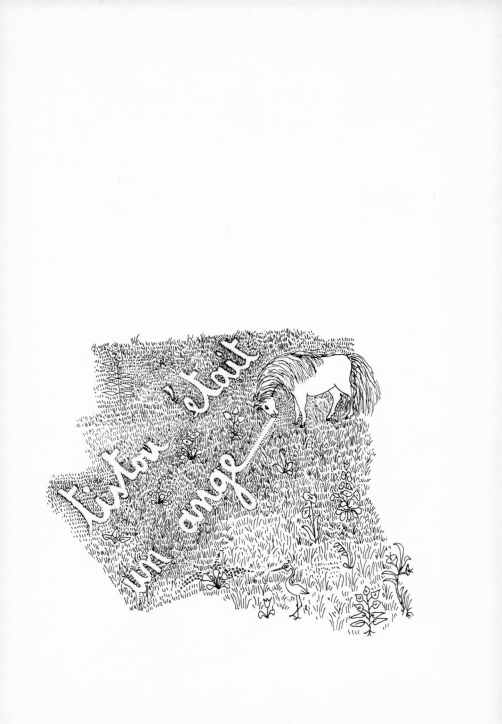